FARTICUS
MAXIMUS

STINK-OFF BATTLE OF THE CENTURY

700038040194

D1341009

For all those who have ever giggled, laughed or snorted
(even a little) at the sound of someone unexpectedly
popping off. This one's for you.   F. A.

Scholastic Children's Books
A division of Scholastic Ltd
Euston House, 24 Eversholt Street
London, NW1 1DB, UK
Registered office: Westfield Road, Southam, Warwickshire, CV47 0RA
SCHOLASTIC and associated logos are trademarks and/or registered
trademarks of Scholastic Inc.

First published in Australia by Scholastic Australia, 2009
This edition published in the UK by Scholastic Ltd, 2011

Text and illustrations copyright © Felice Arena, 2009
The right of Felice Arena to be identified as the author
of this work has been asserted by him.

ISBN 9781407120560

A CIP catalogue record for this book is available from the British Library.
All rights reserved.
This book is sold subject to the condition that it shall not, by way of trade
or otherwise, be lent, hired out or otherwise circulated in any form of binding
or cover other than that in which it is published. No part of this publication
may be reproduced, stored in a retrieval system, or transmitted in any form or
by any means (electronic, mechanical, photocopying, recording or otherwise)
without the prior written permission of Scholastic Limited.

Printed in the UK by CPI Bookmarque, Croydon.
Papers used by Scholastic Children's Books are made from wood
grown in sustainable forests.

13579108642

This is a work of fiction. Names, characters, places, incidents and dialogues are
products of the author's imagination or are used fictitiously. Any resemblance
to actual people, living or dead, events or locales is entirely coincidental.

www.scholastic.co.uk/zone

FARTICUS MAXIMUS

STINK-OFF BATTLE OF THE CENTURY

AND MORE STORIES THAT REEK!

WRITTEN & ILLUSTRATED BY

FELICE ARENA

SCHOLASTIC

CONTENTS

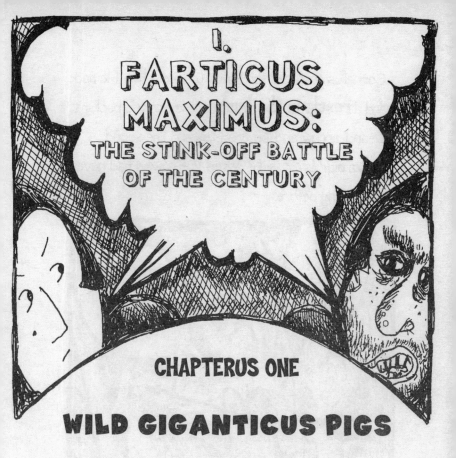

I.
FARTICUS MAXIMUS:
THE STINK-OFF BATTLE OF THE CENTURY

CHAPTERUS ONE

WILD GIGANTICUS PIGS

In the middle of a thick, wooded forest on the outskirts of the bustling, grand ancient city of Rome, two teenage boys were hunting for wild pigs.

'Shuush,' whispered Cornelius, the older of the two.

'What?' croaked Rufus, Cornelius's cousin, who was visiting from the southern city of Pompeii.

1

Cornelius gestured for Rufus to follow him. He had heard a **rustle in the bushes**. He cocked back his bow-and-arrow and tip toed toward the sound.

'Is it a pig? Is it? Is it?' asked Rufus, who had never been hunting before.

Cornelius shot his cousin a dirty look.

'Sorry,' whispered Rufus.

The boys crouched behind the trunk of a large oak tree. When Cornelius peeked to see his prey, he gasped.

'What? What is it?' asked Rufus, seeing the shock on his cousin's face. **Is it a pig?** Or is it something else? Is it a giganticus killer pig with giganticus tuskuses and fangs and...' Cornelius cupped his hand over Rufus's face.

'Shuttus your biggus mouthus, cousin!' he snapped. 'Or he'll hear you!'

'He? Who's he?' asked Rufus in a mouse-like voice.

Cornelius pulled Rufus in and pointed at what had caught his attention.

There in the middle of the woods sat a man with his hands behind his head, looking up to the treetops.

I don't believe it! That's Farticus Maximus!

'Who is it?' asked Rufus.

'Are you kidding?' choked Cornelius. 'That man is the greatest and smelliest gladiator of all time. He's famous! That's **Farticus Maximus!**'

'Farticus who?' asked Rufus with a blank look on his face.

Cornelius shook his head in disbelief.

'Have you been living in a volcano!?' he scoffed. 'Everyone knows his story ... Everyone!'

'Well, I don't,' shrugged Rufus. 'Tell me...'

'OK, I'll give you the shorticus version, 'cause if he **lets one rippus**, we could be seriously injured. Here goes...'

5

CHAPTERUS TWO

ABOUT FARTICUS: THE SO-CALLED SHORTICUS VERSION

Cornelius took in a huge breath and began to tell his cousin Rufus all he knew about the great Farticus Maximus:

'Farticus was born Barticus Sandals. But as a child everyone soon realized he had a **major farting problem**. So they-'

'Farting? You mean Flaticus?' Rufus butted in. 'We don't say fart in Pompeii, we say flaticus – that's the correct term!'

'Well we say farting in Rome and I think you mean flatus not flaticus!' huffed Cornelius. 'May I go on?'

Rufus nodded.

'So, Barticus had a major farting problem, and they

started calling him Farticus. His wind was **so rotten** and **so strong** that it was difficult for anyone to be near him without being seriously knocked-out or blown away – or both! His mother, Helena Sandals, was forced to make orange-scented snotus-rags for herself and the other members of their family. They'd tie these snotus-rags–

'We call them handkerchiefs in Pompeii,' Rufus
interrupted once again.

'Yeah, well, they're snotus-rags here,' grumbled
Cornelius. 'Anyway, Farticus's family wore them around
their noses to block out Farticus's killer stench. When
Farticus reached our age, his **farts were so bad**,
that the mayor of his village ordered Farticus's dad,

Petercus, to get rid of him. Of course, Farticus's mum couldn't let him do that, so she and Farticus went to live on their own, in an abandoned farmhouse just outside of Rome. Got that so far?'

Rufus nodded. Cornelius continued.

'Farticus soon learnt that he could use his **deadly gas** to hunt for food. He would stun wild animals with his thunder-jolting wind and **butterfly-kiss** them, usually with an almighty **hug to the heart** with his trusty dagger.'

'Hold on!' snorted Rufus. 'Butterfly-kiss them? And hug to the heart? What the. . . ?'

Cornelius explained that whenever he wanted to say 'kill' he'd say 'butterfly-kiss' and if he wanted to say 'stab' he'd say 'hug'.

'Why?' asked Rufus.

'Because everyone in Rome is doing it. It's all the rage at the moment. Don't you know anything? Now can I finish this story?'

9

'There's more?' sighed Rufus. 'I thought you said this was the shorticus version.'

Cornelius glared at his cousin.

'OK, I'll wrap this up … but I don't want you interrupting me again. Got it?'

Rufus nodded and Cornelius sucked in another deep breath and blurted the rest out as fast as he could:

'Farticus found it tough to get a job. One day he met Sinus Blockus, an old man who transported wild animals to the gladiator fights. Sinus was born with a rare nose disease that prevented him from smelling — so of course Farticus's smelly farts **didn't affect him**. Sinus's beautiful daughter Rhina also had the same non-smelling nose disease. When Farticus and Rhina set eyes on each other, they instantly fell in love. Sinus convinced Farticus to use the power of his potent wind and become a **gladiator**. Sinus trained Farticus. Within a year Farticus blew away and butterfly-kissed the best gladiators across the land, including a fierce, ugly one by the name of Black Dog Brutus...'

Cornelius panted heavily. His cheeks were flushed. He took in another gulp of air and went on:

'Farticus became **super-rich and famous**. He later retired and married Rhina. They, together with Sinus and Farticus's mother, all now live on a big farm, not too far from here.

'A few months ago, Farticus and Rhina adopted three orphan boys with farting problems and dreams of being great gladiators themselves. Their names:

Rotteneggus, Odorus, and Stinkius.

'But last week, Black Dog Brutus's brother, **Gassius Brutus**, the great farting gladiator from Britannia, unexpectedly showed up wanting to kill — I mean butterfly-kiss — Farticus for butterfly-kissing his brother. Just as the two gladiators were about to have this humongous battle, Rhina stopped them. To Farticus's surprise, Rhina and Gassius knew each other. They had been boyfriend and girlfriend back in Britannia. And when Gassius found out that Farticus was now married to Rhina, he almost **blew his top off** — and his underpants too! Now he really wanted to butterfly-kiss Farticus. But before any of us could say "Oh-Mama-what-a-smell-o-drama!", the emperor of Rome, Bullius, had caught a whiff of their plans to fight and arranged for them to go head-to-head, or should I say **butt-to-butt**, in the most magnificent stadium in the world — the Colosseum. It's going to be the greatest and stinkiest **battle of the century**. And get this, it's going to take place tomorrow!'

A RECAP FROM THE LAST FARTICUS MAXIMUS STORY...

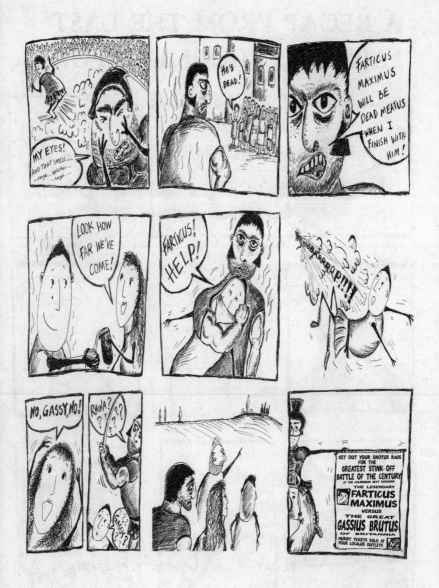

Cornelius collapsed to his knees. Having said so much in so little time had made him feel a little dizzy.

'Woah, that's some story,' gulped Rufus. 'How do you know so much about this guy?'

'I told ya, everyone knows about the great Farticus Maximus. I'm going to hold my nose and go say hello to him. I might try to get his autographus!'

As Cornelius stepped out from behind the tree his jaw dropped. **Farticus was gone!**

'He's left! I've missed my chance! And all because of you! You biggus dufus, Rufus!'

'Me!?' croaked Rufus.

'Yeah, you! If you had known who he was in the first place I wouldn't have wasted my time telling you his story and. . .'

A few hundred metres from where the boys stood, Farticus trudged back toward the city. He could hear the two cousins quarrelling. For a moment he smiled, but then his mind turned back to what he had been thinking about non-stop for the past few days straight

— tomorrow's battle to the death.

Could he beat the great Gassius and secure the heart of his beloved Rhina? Only time would tell.

CHAPTERUS THREE

BRING IT ON!

The following morning the city of Rome was abuzz with excitement. Everyone sensed that this day was definitely going to be one for the history books. Two of the greatest and smelliest gladiators of all time were going to slug it out in an all-out-gas-versus-gas-thunder-cracking-rip-roaring-explosive-butt-wind battle.

Massive crowds flocked to the Colosseum hours before the trumpeters announced the beginning of the fight. Some had desperately tried to get last-minute tickets, but it was no use — this one-off **mega-fartfest** had sold out within an hour.

By the early afternoon the citizens of Rome couldn't contain their excitement. The final countdown to the most fantastical, freakiest fart-fight had begun. In less than an hour Farticus and Gassius would make their way into the famous arena. Everyone had smiles on their faces, even Farticus's mother, Helena.

Helena was very happy. She was making a butterfly-kissing on sales of her orange-scented snotus-rags. Big crowds had swamped the snotus-rag stall she had set up by the entrance of the Colosseum. Most spectators knew the gladiators' stink-wrestle was going to be unbearable — there was no way they were going to risk being gassed.

Some, though, chose to live dangerously.

'Bring it on!' roared one man to his buddy. 'I bet you I won't pass out. Orange-scented snotus-rags are for wimps!'

As the excitement grew above ground, beneath the Colosseum, among the dark stone corridors where the savage man-eating beasts, murderous criminals, and slaves were caged, Farticus was getting ready for the showdown of his life.

'Remember to always keep your eyes on him,' said Sinus, trying his best to rev-up Farticus. 'You can't let him blow you off your feet or he'll **finish you off** with his wham-bam-slam-his-bottomus-on-the-face move. That's his trademark. Got it? Farticus? I said, you got that?'

Farticus wasn't listening to his father-in-law. His mind was a million miles away. He hadn't even realized that he had popped-off several times in a row and knocked out the two soldiers guarding his cell. Sinus **slapped** Farticus across the face.

'Snap out of it, son! You haven't fought for over a year, so you have to trust me and listen to my advice! Your life is at stake here!'

'Why should

You have to focus! Your life is at stake here!

I trust you?' scoffed Farticus as he put on his body armour. 'You never bothered to tell me that Rhina had been engaged to Gassius before she met me.'

'Oh, are you still going on about that?!' huffed Sinus. 'We told you, that was a long time ago. Rhina didn't want to marry him. It was a **biggus mistakus**. She's married to you now. She loves you, not him! You love her, don't you?'

'Of course!'

'And you would do anything to keep that love alive, wouldn't you?'

Farticus nodded.

'Then stopping being a baby. Show how much she truly means to you and blow that **rotten gas-bag** from Britannia away. Remember, you are the great Farticus Maximus!'

Farticus knew Sinus was right. He had to prove his love for Rhina and get rid of the evil Gassius once and for all.

CHAPTERUS FOUR

MAN-EATING BIG CATS

'Father-farter! Father-farter!' came the excited voices echoing off the stone corridor walls.

It was Farticus's three adopted sons, Rotteneggus, Odorus, and Stinkius, bursting into their father's changing cell, all three with orange-scented snotus-rags tied around their faces.

'What are you boys doing here?'

'We just met Emperor Bullius's best friend and personal assistant, General Yesmanus!' croaked Odorus.

'He let us down here once he was told we were your sons,' added Stinkius.

'He said he could make us gladiators one day,' exclaimed Rotteneggus. 'And he said he could make us rich and really, really famous like you and take us to visit the palace if we liked and...'

'OK, you boys are getting way too excited!' chimed in Sinus. 'Your father needs to get ready. Go on back to your seats in the stadium.'

Farticus embraced his sons. **BBBRRRPPP!** They all farted in unison and laughed.

'There's another reason why you need to focus,' Sinus whispered in Farticus's ear. 'You have to do it for them! These boys look up to you! You're not just their father, **you're their hero!'**

Farticus stuck out his chest proudly, placed his helmet on his head, and ripped out one more pre-fight nervous-stinker. This was the moment.

As the boys ran off, Farticus and Sinus made their way to the iron gates that opened out into the arena. The crowd cheered and roared loudly. The pre-fight entertainment had already begun. Farticus watched from the shadows.

Ten criminals were released into the arena. The crowd roared and booed. The criminals had no armour or weapons, and huddled together like frightened lambs. Suddenly, from the tunnel opposite to where Farticus was waiting, ten fierce, hungry lions and tigers were released into the arena.

The crowd cheered. The criminals were trapped.
Arm in arm they shuffled to the centre of the arena.
The lions and tigers roared and then charged for the
criminals. Again, the crowd cheered. This was going to
be ugly and bloody — ugly and bloody indeed. Farticus
found it tough to watch. One tiger pounced on two
criminals at one time and **bit their heads off**.
Another poor slave was about to be mauled by a tiger
that had grabbed his hands and a lion that had him by
the feet. Talk about a gruesome way to go.

After the man-eating big cats had butterfly-kissed all the criminals, the arena was cleared and made ready for the **main event**: Farticus versus Gassius.

A band of soldiers blew their trumpets to herald the entrance of the gassy gladiators. The iron gate opened and Farticus slowly stepped out onto the sunlit surface of the arena. The entire stadium **erupted**. Everyone roared and stomped their feet. Their deafening cheers could be heard all over the city of Rome.

'Long live Farticus! Long live Farticus!' they chanted.

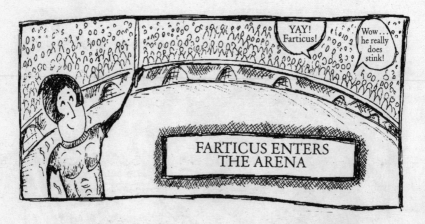

FARTICUS ENTERS
THE ARENA

A few moments later, Gassius Brutus made his entrance from a gate at the opposite end of the stadium. The crowd **hissed** and **booed**. Farticus was clearly their favourite. Gassius snarled and waved his sword at the spectators, as if to say 'I don't care.'

AS DOES THE
GREAT GASSIUS

The two gladiators met in the centre and sized each other up. They raised their swords to Emperor Bullius and waited for his signal to begin fighting.

A few rows behind the emperor sat Farticus's mother and his three smelly adopted sons. They waved at him. He waved back. Farticus then spotted Rhina, who blew him a kiss. Just as Farticus was about to return her greeting he caught sight of Gassius blowing a kiss and bowing in her direction. Farticus became even

more furious when Gassius turned and smirked and snorted at him.

The emperor raised his hand. The crowd roared again. The fight was on.

CHAPTERUS FiVE

THE BATTLE OF ALL BATTLES

Gassius wasted no time when it came to inflicting the first blow.

BBBRRRRRRPPPPPPPP!!!!!!

Farticus was instantly blown off his feet. The crowd booed.

'Woah, that had some kick to it,' Farticus coughed, wobbling back up on to his feet.

BBBRRRRRRPPPPPPPP!!!!!!

Gassius struck again. Farticus hit the sandy arena with a thud.

'BOOOOOO!!!' hissed the crowd.

'LOOK OUT!!!' some of them screamed.

Farticus looked up to see Gassius **flying through the air** at him bottomus-first.

'Oh, no!' gulped Farticus. 'He's trying his trademark manoeuvre. The wham-bam-slam-his-bottomus-on-the-face move!'

Farticus quickly rolled over onto his stomach, pointed his bottomus toward Gassius, and,

BBBRRRRRRPPPPPPPP!!!!!!

Farticus **shot Gassius down** in mid-air. His opponent was catapulted to the ground with a huge thump.

The crowd cheered as their hero sprang to his feet.

'You are **SO dead meatus** for doing that!' growled Gassius, brushing the dust off his armour.

He is SO dead meatus for doing that!

The great stink-off showdown was turning out to be the battle of all battles. Back and forth the smelly gladiators blew each other off their feet. But neither seemed able to get the advantage and end it with a final, deadly blow.

It wasn't long before Farticus and Gassius realized that their farts were **useless against each other**. They were evenly matched. So they put down their bottomusses and resorted to good old-fashioned fighting — no gas — just plain old gladiator wrestling.

In a sudden surge, Gassius got Farticus in a headlock. Farticus gasped for air as Gassius tightened his bulging biceps around his throat. Gassius raised his sword, ready to **hug** Farticus in the lower back. The crowd gasped.

'No!' cried Rhina, her hands over her eyes.

Was this **the end** for Farticus?

WHACK!!!!!

Farticus jabbed his elbow backwards and thumped Gassius below the belt.

Gassius released his grip and keeled over. The crowd screamed their delight. Rhina let out a huge sigh of relief.

As Farticus tried to suck some air back into his lungs, he saw all the gates swinging open. Within moments fifty blood-thirsty **wild animals** had entered the arena.

'What the . . . ?' gulped Farticus, as five tigers, fifteen lions, five bulls, five rhinoceroses, ten wolves, and ten grizzly bears had all locked eyes on him.

Pettleton,' she adds, turning to me. 'Are you hungry?'

I nod.

'Well, we're going to stop at the next roadside restaurant, OK?'

Great, I thought. I couldn't wait to get out. The last time we stopped was about three hours ago.

'Are you having fun, son?' my dad asks.

It's about the twentieth time he's asked me that on this trip. And I know why. He knows that deep down I think **road trips suck** — especially really long road trips. Just once I wish we would fly. But my dad hates flying. Actually, my dad can't stand a lot of things, but not in normal ways like everyone else.

He gets really weird about a lot of things. For instance, he hates flying; not because he's scared that the plane might drop out of the sky, but because he needs to breathe fresh air, not cabin air with a million other passengers' germs flying around him.

I heard my mum say once that it's the quirky things that she loves about Dad. And I have to agree with her.

Even the crowd had been taken by surprise. They all gasped, before breaking out in chants of. . .

'BLOOD! BLOOD! BLOOD!'

'BUTTERFLY-KISS! BUTTERFLY-KISS!'

and

'GO, ANIMALS, GO!'

Farticus turned to Gassius, who was still writhing on the ground.

'What's going on?' he asked.

'It's an **ambush!**' croaked Gassius.

'A what?'

'It's an ambush!' repeated Gassius. 'Emperor Bullius doesn't want either of us to win. He wants to see us **both dead**. We've been set up!'

WILL BULLIUS GET HIS
WAY AND SEE THE END OF
FARTICUS AND GASSIUS?

OR WILL FARTICUS AND
GASSIUS COMBINE THEIR
DEADLY WINDUS AND TAKE
ON THE EVILUS EMPEROR?

FIND OUT IN THE EXCITING
CONCLUSION AT THE
END OF THIS BOOK:
FARTICUS MAXIMUS:
SILENTUS BUT DEADLIUS

11. LITTLE OLD GRANNIES DON'T TOOT!

'Well, hello Sleepyhead!'

'Where are we?' I mumble, looking out of the back-seat window of our car.

'We're exactly five-hundred-and-twenty-two kilometres away from home!' answers my dad, grinn[...] at me through the rear-view mirror.

'Oh, Nigel, stop it!' my mum quips, lightly slapping [...] father on the shoulder.

'We've just gone through a cute little town calle[...]

Dad just wouldn't be Dad without his quirky ways. But sometimes it can be annoying.

Take farting, for instance. My dad hates anything to do with farting. He even hates the word. If I have to say it, he makes me say things like **toot**, or **expel gas**, or he'd even accept **break wind**.

As for actually letting one rip, well, you can't, not around him, that's for sure. Otherwise, he loses it. He goes totally berserk, which sometimes is a little scary.

That's why I can't wait until we get to this roadside restaurant. I really want to **squeeze one out**. My stomach is doing backflips. Five hours in a car without being allowed to pop off, even with the windows down, is torture.

By the way, I once farted, I mean tooted, in the car and Dad kicked me out. Right there in front of my school, in front of all my friends. I had to catch the bus home. Seriously. See, weird. But we all have weird, quirky things about us, don't we?

'Yeah, it's fun! This trip is great!' I lie to my dad, as we

finally pull-in to the roadside restaurant.

I hop out of the car and bolt to the toilets as if I were in the track and field 100-metre Olympic final.

I slam the toilet door behind me, and

BBBRRRRRRPPPPPPPP!!!!!!

Ahhh, I sigh. I so needed to do that. My entire body is thanking me, especially my stomach. In fact, I let another one go:

BBBRRRRRRPPPPPPPP!!!!!!

'Hamish!' roars my dad, coming into the toilet. 'That's disgusting!'

'Sorry!' I say, even though I'm not.

I mean, seriously, if you can't let fluffy off the chain in the privacy of your own toilet stall, where else can you?

'Can you try to pass your gas **quietly** please, Hamish,' adds my dad. 'It really sounds disgusting!'

'OK, only super quiet ones,' I say sarcastically. 'So only dogs can hear 'em!'

'Don't be smart!' snaps my dad.

For a moment I think that if my dad could, he would kick me out of the toilets as punishment. But he knows he can't. That would be too weird even for him. It's not like I'm in the back seat of the car — thank goodness!

When Dad and I return to Mum we find her speaking to a little grey-haired old lady.

'This is Mrs Butterworth,' says my mum. 'Her car has broken down and she was wondering if we could give her a lift to her town, which is only twenty minutes away. I said that it would be OK.'

'Um, excuse us just for a moment,' my dad coughs.

Dad drags my mother and me aside.

'Um, you know how I feel about picking up strangers,' he whispers to my mum.

'She's an old woman, Nigel, not a serial killer! And she needs our help!'

'Yes, but what if she does a . . .'

I know what my dad is thinking. I can also tell that my mum also knows what he is about to say.

'Nigel, you've got to be kidding,' says my mother. 'She won't pass gas!'

'Yeah, Dad!' I chime in. **Little old grannies don't toot!**

'OK, then,' sighs my dad, backing down. 'But if she does...'

Mum rolls her eyes and invites Mrs Butterworth to jump into the back seat with me.

'So, how old are you?' she asks me.

'Eleven.'

'And are you enjoying your school holidays?'

'Yes.'

So far, so good. I think Mrs Butterworth is very nice in a grandmotherly way. It's nice to have someone else to talk to on this trip. I catch Mum smiling at me and see that Dad still looks nervous in the rear-view mirror.

Suddenly, **I smell something.** At first it smells like eggs, then wet smelly socks, and then eggs in wet smelly socks. I don't believe it. I think Mrs Butterworth just did a **silent but deadly** one. I panic. I quickly wind down the window, hoping my dad won't smell it. But it's too late. The stench is so strong it hits my folks fair across the nostrils. Dad slams on the brakes.

'WHO DID THAT?' he roars, pulling up on the side of the road. 'HAMISH?'

I want to take the hit for the sweet Mrs Butterworth and just as I'm about to say it was me — she confesses it was her.

'I'm so sorry,' she says, blushing as bright as a beetroot. 'I've been a little under the weather. Must be the medicine I'm taking. I do apologize.'

'**OUT!**' my dad yells.

'Excuse me?' gulps Mrs Butterworth, looking confused.

'Nigel, you can't!' cries my mother.

'I said **GET OUT! GET OUT, NOW!**

Mrs Butterworth reluctantly hops out of the car. I can tell she is shocked and terrified by my father's crazy response. She looks at me briefly, to see if this is some kind of joke.

I shrug and give her a look as if to say, 'I'm sorry, it's not,' and, 'Please forgive him, that's just the way he is.'

Dad speeds off, leaving her stranded in the middle of nowhere.

How dare she! my dad mumbles angrily under his breath. 'And you said that little old ladies don't toot. Huh!'

Shaking her head, my mother is so upset with Dad that she's lost for words. I look back to see that Mrs Butterworth is waving at us.

'Is she gesturing towards us?!' my dad growls, looking back through the rear-view mirror.

'No, I think she's just shooing away some flies,' I lie, relieved to see another car pulling up to help her out.

We drive for an hour without any of us saying a word. The tension is pretty thick. I really hate road trips.

'What's this now?' my dad moans, breaking the silence.

He slows the car to a stop. Mum and I sit up to see a very pretty woman standing in the middle of the road waving us down. She's wearing a gold sparkly dress as if she were about to walk down the red carpet of a Hollywood movie premiere. In fact, she looks as if she could be a Hollywood star.

'Oh, please, please help me!' she cries, leaning into Dad's window. 'My boyfriend kicked me out of the car!'

I was about to say, *you didn't fart, did you?* But I didn't.

'We had this huge argument,' she adds. 'And anyway I need to urgently get to the next town because I'm the reigning **beauty queen**, and I'm presenting an award at this year's top model contest. Please, can you take me?'

'Um, excuse us for a moment,' my dad says, winding up the window so the beauty queen can't hear us.

'I'm not sure about this, what if she. . .'

'I'm staying right out of this one!' snaps my mum, folding her arms and looking the other way.

She's still mad with my dad.

'Dad,' I say, 'She's a beauty queen. **Beauty queens don't toot!**'

Dad glares back at me. I know what he's thinking,

45

and I quickly think of something else to say.

'I mean, she doesn't look like she would be a farter, I mean a tooter, I mean a wind-breaker, whatever! Come on Dad, you have to help her. Look, she's crying.'

The beauty queen did have tears in her eyes. Dad can't be that mean. He agrees to take her.

Like Mrs Butterwoth, the beauty queen is very nice. She even smells really nice. I can tell that the strong but alluring perfume she's wearing has calmed Dad's nerves down a bit — even Mum's looking happier.

Mum talks to the beauty queen about her dress and her hair and all that girly stuff.

'Um, just turn right here, please,' says the beauty queen, as we drive into the next town.

'And then the next left. Then it should only be another couple of hundred metres or so down on the right,' she adds, directing Dad.

Finally we turn into the street where the event is being held, but without any warning the beauty queen rips out a humongous cracker.

BBBRRRRPPPPPPPPPPPPPPP!!!!!!

It's so loud, it's as if someone had shot off a rifle inside the car. My jaw drops. I can't believe it. I snort nervously. There's no way she can pretend it isn't her. My dad slams on the brakes!

'I'm so sorry,' giggles the beauty queen, totally embarrassed. 'Must be nerves. I thought I could **squeak out a quiet one**. I'm so sorry!'

'**GET OUT!**' screams my dad.

'But you can't expect me to walk in these heels all the way...'

'I said, **GET OUT! GET OUT, NOW!** No-one expels gas in my car! Get out!'

I wave goodbye to the beauty queen, but she doesn't wave back. She also makes a sign with her hand as we drive off.

And once again there's silence in the car, but not for long.

'You've got to be joking,' grumbles my dad, as yet

another figure standing in the middle of the road waves us down.

This time it's a truck driver.

'Thanks for stopping. My truck has broken down. Can you drop me off at the next town?'

'No!' says my dad straight out.

Mum and I say nothing. If grannies and beauty queens can let one rip then it wouldn't take a genius to work out that truck drivers can too. In fact, I'm guessing that truck drivers are the **kings of letting them rip**. I don't like this guy's chances.

'Why not?' asks the truck driver.

'Because,' says my father. 'I don't want to!'

'Look, buddy, I've been stranded here for over two hours, I really need your help!'

'Well, I wish I could help but. . .'

I notice my mum wriggling in her seat. She blurts: 'My husband can't take you sir, because he's afraid you might break wind!'

Dad huffs and shoots a dirty look at Mum.

'Well, he's got nothing to worry about!' exclaims the truck driver. 'Yes, I break wind if I have to, but never in the company of others. In fact, I think that **passing gas** in general **is disgusting**. I would never do that! You have my word!'

Before I can even say I think Dad has just found his quirky twin, we are on the move again with the truck driver now sitting next to me.

And like Mrs Butterworth and the beauty queen he's very friendly. He and Dad talk for ages about other things in life they can't stand, and how some people judge them for it. Mum and I roll our eyes at each other.

I look out of my window and zone out for a while. I see that the sun has set and that it will be dark very soon. The truck driver and Dad have now stopped talking. Everyone's quiet. And I think we're all happy about that.

A few minutes later and I see that Mum has dozed off. I can tell this because her bottom lip has dropped and I can see a little dribble on the corner of her mouth. I smile. But I also feel my eyelids getting heavy. Everything is getting blurry. Ahh, sleep. Yeah, I'm gonna sleep now.

'Well, here we are!' I hear as I slowly wake up and see the truck driver hopping out of our car.

'Are we here already?' Mum mumbles, also just waking up.

'Yes, we are, you two were out for an hour!' says Dad.

'Well, thank you for helping me out,' says the truck driver, sticking his head back into the car. 'And by the way, I'm not sure if I should say this but while you two were asleep the driver here passed gas. It was **loud and vulgar**. And frankly, I was deeply offended by it. But I'm thankful that you helped me out. See ya and have a great trip!'

The truck driver slams the car door shut. I look at Mum and we then turn to see Dad, grinning nervously. We can't believe what we just heard — **Dad tooted?**

'Um, look, I know what you're both thinking,' stutters my dad. 'And, well, you were all asleep and. . .'

I'm sure Dad can see the steam coming out of our ears. There's nothing else we can say but:

GET OUT! GET OUT! GET OUT, NOW!

III. STINKLOCK HOLMES: THE HUNT FOR LADY WINNIE WINSTON'S WIND-BREAKER

On a foggy Monday afternoon in London in the year 1889 a rather plump man in a long dark coat approached a grand building opposite the Baker Street underground station.

After knocking urgently on the door, the man paused to read the plaque hanging to the right of the entrance, by the front window.

'Hello, how can I help you?' asked **Dr Buttson**,

Welcome to the residence
of England's Greatest Detective:
STINKLOCK HOLMES
and his trusty companion,
Dr John Buttson.
Available to solve all types of cases:
big or small, sweet or rotten.
ENQUIRE WITHIN.

warmly greeting the man in the long coat.

'I was wondering if I could see Mr Holmes? I have a very important message to deliver to him.'

'Well, you've caught him in the middle of his afternoon tea break. If you'd like to return at a more suitable time I'm sure...'

'That's fine, my dear Buttson, I can see the gentleman now,' echoed a deep voice from the hallway.

It was **Stinklock Holmes** himself — a tall, handsome man wearing a three-piece tweed suit and smoking an impressive, curved calabash pipe.

'What can I do for you?' asked the famous detective as he stepped up beside Buttson.

'My name is Rupert James. I'm the head butler at the Winston estate. Lady Winnie Winston has sent me to call on your services, sir. It is of utmost importance.'

'Well, what's the problem?'

The butler went on to tell Stinklock that he wasn't able to say. Lady Winston had simply requested that Mr Holmes come to call on her as soon as possible. She lived in a large manor in the Berkshire countryside, but for the past week was staying in London — in her Knightsbridge residence.

'I have a hansom cab waiting out front, sir,' added the butler.

'Then **what are we waiting for?**' exclaimed Stinklock enthusiastically.

'But Holmes,' coughed Buttson. 'What about your tea?'

'I can always whip up my own special brew for you,

Mr Holmes, when we get to Knightsbridge,' interjected the butler.

'Perfect!' roared Stinklock. 'Buttson, grab me my hat and cloak! Off we go!'

Buttson glared at the butler as he fetched Stinklock's trademark deerstalker hat and riding cloak.

When the three men arrived at the Winston residence, Lady Winnie swooped down the grand staircase looking **terribly flushed**.

'Mr Holmes, thank you for coming so promptly!'

'The pleasure is all mine, my lady,' bowed Stinklock. 'This is my trusty companion, Dr Buttson.'

'Hello.'

'Hello.'

'So, my lady, what seems to be the problem?' asked Stinklock. 'Your butler said it was extremely urgent.'

'I'm not sure how I can say this without sounding **vulgar**,' Lady Winnie stuttered. 'But before I go on, Rupert, please fetch us some refreshments; tea perhaps. All right then, where was I? Oh, yes, here goes...'

Lady Winnie took in a deep breath.

'As you may or may not know, Mr Holmes, I have a reputation for holding the grandest candlelit dinner parties in all of England.'

'Yes, I've heard,' said Stinklock, nodding.

'Well, my reputation is at stake, Mr Holmes,' said Lady Winnie, her voice cracking as if she were about to cry. 'On Saturday night during pre-dinner drinks, a **rotten, lingering smell** filled the room. It hit us like a northerly wind off the Thames. The odour was so vulgar it made many of my guests quite queasy. Some, dare I say, wanted to throw up. Of course, I shuffled everyone out as quickly as I could into another room, but by then the damage had been done!'

'My lady, may I ask, what was the rotten stench?'

'Well, I'm embarrassed to say!' exclaimed Lady Winnie. 'But it's obvious, isn't it? One of my guests dropped a foul and **dirty rotten stinker!**'

'And?' said Stinklock, not sure how to respond.

'And...' added Lady Winnie, 'I want you to find out

who it was, and **expose the gassy culprit**.

Stinklock was confused.

'Why?' he asked. 'What would be the purpose of that, my lady? What's done is done, no? And may I say that your residence now smells as fresh as a meadow of spring flowers!'

Lady Winnie pursed her lips and shook her head in frustration.

'Mr Holmes, I fear that you fail to see the seriousness of all of this. The talk of my smelly party is spreading across greater London right now as we speak — if no explanation is provided, no-one will come to any of my parties in the future...'

The butler shuffled in with a pot of tea and a silver platter stacked with shortbread.

'Now, you'll love this brew, sir,' he grinned at Stinklock, placing the tray on a nearby stand. 'I suspect it may even be better than the one you usually have at home.'

The butler smirked at Buttson.

Buttson pulled a face in return.

Lady Winnie continued.

'The standard of my exclusive gatherings has been shattered with one foul and revolting pop-off. The only way to save my reputation is to reveal the identity of the **nasty wind-breaker** and to publicly ban him or her from future parties. That's the only thing that will ensure that my guests return.'

'Well, what are we waiting for?' asked Stinklock, taking a swig of tea and returning the cup to the butler. 'Take me to the room where the crime, I mean, the incident, occurred.'

Lady Winnie led the way. Stinklock followed, with Buttson pacing closely beside him.

'Sir, I bet the tea wasn't as good as mine,' he whispered.

Stinklock rolled his eyes and chose not to respond to Buttson.

'Right, this is the room,' announced Lady Winnie.

Stinklock asked her to name the guests and where they had been standing at the time the silent but deadly wind was released.

'Well, I was standing here talking to Baron Von Razberri. Dame Widebottom was deep in conversation with Sir Reekston by the piano. And my remaining guests, Baroness Skidmarkton, Duke Poopoffton, and the French ambassador, Monsieur Tootin le Pants were all over there by the fireplace. Oh, and of course, there was Rupert, serving us all.'

'Hmmm,' mumbled Stinklock, his mind already racing.

'And who was the first to raise the alarm?' he asked. 'That is, who was it that **smelt the stench first?** Was it you, my lady?'

'No. I had stepped out and it was upon my return that I found my guests **coughing, spluttering**, and **complaining** about the rotten gas.'

'Oh, so you weren't actually in the room at the time the wind was released?' pressed Stinklock. 'Why not?'

'Well, I had popped out to the kitchen to fetch more champagne.'

'Oh, I see,' hummed Stinklock.

Rupert the butler then came back into the room to tell Lady Winston that someone was waiting for her in the front hallway.

Lady Winston excused herself and left Stinklock to ponder the mystery.

'Ah, Rupert, may I ask you something?' Stinklock called out to the butler.

'You don't want more of his tea, do you, sir?' quipped Buttson, looking terribly irritated.

Stinklock again rolled his eyes at his trusty but overly-sensitive companion.

'Yes Mr Holmes, what is it you want to know?' asked the butler.

'Lady Winston said she was out of the room at the time the foul wind was let loose. Where were you?'

'I was serving Monsieur Tootin le Pants.'

Stinklock moved over to the fireplace.

'He was standing with Baroness Skidmarkton and Duke Poopoffton, with their backs to the fireplace, correct?'

'Yes,' answered the butler.

'And who was the first among the guests to bring **attention to the smell?'**

'Well,' said the butler. 'I think it was Baron Von Razberri. Yes, I remember it was he who raised the alarm. He has a booming voice, you see, and I had turned to see what all the commotion was about.'

Stinklock took a few paces to where Baron Von Razberri would have been standing.

'And I suspect,' he pressed on, 'that the next couple of guests to raise a fuss were Dame Widebottom and Sir Reekston, yes?'

The butler agreed.

'And finally, I'm guessing you and the three guests by the fireplace were the last to smell the offending odour. Correct?'

The butler nodded again.

'So, we can assume that the rotten stench,' remarked Stinklock, with an excited tone in his voice, 'originated from somewhere around Baron Von Razberri and

drifted diagonally **across the room** toward the fireplace.'

'So, Holmes,' Buttson coughed in. 'Are you saying that our wind-breaker is Baron Von Razberri, since that's where the stench was first smelt? Was he trying to **throw us off the scent**, so to speak?'

'Well, it would appear so, my dear Buttson,' sighed Stinklock. 'But as you know, in the world of investigation nothing is ever what it seems.'

'Um, excuse me, sir,' interrupted Rupert. 'If you won't be needing me any more I must attend to a couple of things in the grand hall.'

Stinklock nodded, but then called out: 'Oh, I do have one more question for you!'

The butler turned to Stinklock. 'Yes?'

'Was the fire in the fireplace a roaring, high-flaming fire or was it a little, crackling one?'

'Hmm,' thought the butler. 'I recall it was a small, crackling one.'

'And at the time the foul wind was broken, was it still a small, crackling one?'

'I'm not quite sure. But I think so.'

The butler left the room and Buttson rushed to Stinklock's side.

'You already know who the **mystery wind-breaker** is, don't you, Holmes?' he asked excitedly.

Stinklock nodded.

'It's Baron Von Razberri, isn't it?'

Stinklock shook his head.

'Then **it has to be the butler**,' added Buttson. 'It's always the butler! I knew it! This one has shifty eyes and boasts way too much about his fancy tea. My brew is way better than his!'

'No, my dear Buttson.' Stinklock smiled at his friend as Lady Winnie glided back in to the room. 'It's not the butler,' he whispered, 'but you will find out very soon.'

'Well, my reputation is already in tatters,' cried Lady Winnie, throwing her hands into the air. 'That was the butler of the Indonesian Foreign Secretary's wife, Dame Poopoocaca, calling to decline the invitation to my next party. See, the damage has been done, Mr Holmes. I need you to find the dirty wind-breaker at once!'

Stinklock took a step towards Lady Winnie and calmly said: 'I have, my lady.'

'You have?' gasped Lady Winnie. 'Well, you are a fast worker, indeed. Who was it then? I bet it was Baron Von Razberri or Dame Sidebottom. She was stuffing her mouth with peanuts as soon as she stepped through the front door!'

'No, my Lady, it was neither Baron Von Razberri nor the peanut-loving Dame Sidebottom, nor any of your guests for that matter,' croaked Stinklock. 'In fact, the dirty rotten wind-breaker was . . . you!'

Lady Winnie slapped Stinklock across the face. **'How dare you!'** she snarled.

'I will ignore that,' said Stinklock, rubbing his cheek, 'only because you most likely acted purely out of embarrassment. But please grant me the privilege of explaining why I think you were the culprit.'

Lady Winnie was seething, but she nodded for Stinklock to continue.

'I surmised very quickly that the stench must have originated from somewhere near where Baron Von Razberri had been standing. And then it wafted its way toward the fireplace.

'Actually, if any of the guests who had been standing by the fireplace had passed gas, I'm quite sure such a powerful stinker would have caused the flames in the fireplace to flare up. As we all know, **toxic gas** combined with **flames** is a **dangerous mix**.

'But your butler said there were no sudden bursts of large flames throughout this entire stinky incident.'

Dr Buttson nodded along with Stinklock.

'So, it could not have been any of the guests by the fireplace,' Stinklock reiterated. 'As for the guests in the middle of the room, well, they were caught in the crossfire. They reacted after Baron Von Razberri!'

'But then don't you see? It had to be him, not me!' snapped Lady Winnie.

'Well, that is what I thought at first ... until you let something very significant slip, my lady.'

'And what was that?'

'You mentioned that you had left the room to fetch more champagne.'

'Yes, so ... what's so strange about that?' asked Lady Winnie, defiantly.

'My lady, you have a butler to fetch champagne. And as far as I know, in society, the lady of the house never has to fetch a thing.'

The colour drained out of Lady Winnie's face. Stinklock was close to wrapping this up.

'Could it be that you dropped a **silent but deadly stinker** and didn't want anyone to suspect it was you?' he proposed. 'The only thing you could possibly do was leave the room as swiftly as possible — hence the feeble excuse about fetching champagne. So poor old Baron Von Razberri, who had been standing closest to you, was the first to cop your rotten stench and sound the alarm. But of course he ended up taking the blame. My compliments, Lady Winnie. It was a great cover-up and it allowed you to casually return a few moments later and pretend to be horrified.'

Lady Winnie slumped into a nearby chair and dropped her face into the palms of her hands.

'Yes! Yes! It was me! It was me all along!' she sobbed. 'I'm the dirty rotten wind-breaker! My life is over!'

Stinklock moved toward Lady Winnie and gently put his hand on her shoulder.

'My lady, if it's any consolation, **everyone breaks wind**. I'm sure the Queen herself lets one rip every now and then.'

'Oh, please!' cried Lady Winnie, her eyes now filled with tears. 'What about my dinner parties? I live for them, and now no-one will want to come!'

As Lady Winnie sobbed Stinklock noticed a dog sleeping soundly in the corner of the room.

'Ah, Lady Winnie, **is that your dog?**'

Lady Winnie looked to where Stinklock was pointing.

'Of course it's my dog. It's my beloved Italian greyhound, Lorenzo. Bless the old dear. That's his favourite spot. He sleeps there all day and night long.'

Stinklock smiled at Buttson. He had a brilliant idea.

On the ride back home, Buttson couldn't stop praising Stinklock.

'Sir, I just can't say it enough,' he beamed proudly. 'Suggesting that Lady Winnie write to her guests to say that her beloved Lorenzo was the source of the foul stench — and that at future parties the poor dog would be tied up outside... Just brilliant!'

'Elementary, my dear Buttson,' grinned Stinklock. 'It's the oldest and **most reliable excuse in the book** — blame the dog. I'm sure Lady Winnie's reputation will remain intact.

'But now that's over, you know what I'm in the mood for, my dear friend?'

'No. What?' asked Buttson.

'A pot of your tea. I didn't care much for the butler's brew!'

'Oh, sir, that's music to my ears.'

'Hello, Ben! Are you OK? We saw you on the news!'

'Yeah, I'm OK. I'm glad to be home!'

It was true. I couldn't be happier to be home, safe and sound back in my bedroom with all my stuff around me.

'OK, thanks Gran, bye!'

That was like the tenth call since getting back this afternoon. It seemed as if everyone had seen me and my friends on TV.

'Ben? You star! You made the news! What happened?'

Here I go again. It's David, my cousin. We act more like best friends than cousins. We're the same age.

David tells me he wants to know every single detail and how I ended up on the news. He pushes me to start from the beginning, which is probably as good a place as any...

It all began two days ago when my class headed out on a school camp. We all boarded the bus that was to take us on a four-hour journey to Gunder National Park.

My friends Johnno, Tubs, Marty and I made sure we got the back seats. Everyone on the bus was really excited. We all talked over the top of each other about anything and everything. We hadn't even noticed the towns we passed through.

Toward the end of our trip Johnno cried out:

PHWWWOOHH! Someone just let one rip! It's rotten!'

Like a domino effect everyone on the bus, including

the driver and the teachers, were hit by the foul-wafting stench.

'That's disgusting!'

'That's not right!'

'Woah, that's serious stinkage!'

'Who did it?'

'Not me!'

'Not me!'

'Don't look at me!'

'It wasn't me!'

Once the smell disappeared everyone settled down, except for us four sitting in the back seats.

'Tubs, fess up! That was you, wasn't it?' said Johnno pointing the finger at him.

Tubs is blamed for a lot of things. I suppose he's **always eating** and when it comes to passing gas, well, let's just say that those two things always go hand in hand.

'No way! I swear!' he coughed. 'I swear on this deliciously doughy doughnut with mouth-watering chocolate icing and sprinkles on top!'

'Then if it wasn't Tubs, it had to be either you Ben, or you Marty!'

'It wasn't me! It's mathematically impossible that I would've done it,' protested Marty.

Marty's the smartest kid in our class, possibly the entire school.

'If you had noticed I was sitting on the left-hand side of you, Johnno, and when you were hit by the smell you were facing the right-hand side,' he said. 'Which means if you calculate the angle and the trajectory of the waft with the moment it hit your nostrils, anyone with a brain could tell you it couldn't possibly have been me! In fact, maybe it was you! Maybe it's a case of **he who smelt it, dealt it!**'

'Yeah, right! It wasn't me, brainiac! Besides, I would've said it was me. You know how I love to… **PHWWWOOHH!** Someone just dropped another one!'

It was true. The silent but deadly gas was back — and it was more **potent** and **rotten** than the last. Again, the bus erupted into moans and groans of disgust.

Fortunately, we had made it to our destination and everyone piled off the bus coughing and spluttering for fresh air just before we all passed out.

It wasn't long before we soon forgot about the smell; we were all too excited to finally be at our campsite. The teachers divided us into groups of four — the number assigned to each cabin.

Luckily Tubs, Johnno, Marty and I were all put together. While we unpacked our stuff in our cabin, I darted off to the communal toilets. I was desperate to go — **number two was calling**. But nothing. False alarm. When I got back to my cabin, my friends were all facing the door, as if they were waiting for me.

'It was you, **you big stinker!**' snapped Johnno. 'You're the one who gassed out the bus!'

I was going to say no, but the expression on my face was already saying yes. I couldn't lie, 'cause Johnno was right. It had been me all along.

My friends teased and joked with me for the next couple of minutes. But they warned that I'd be kicked out in a flash if I let one loose in the cabin.

'OK,' I said. 'It's not like I can control it, but I'll do my best to keep our cabin **deadly-gas free**.'

Several minutes later we all gathered with our fellow classmates for our first camp activity — a contest called the Orientation Hike Race.

Teamed up in our cabin groups, with a map in hand, we were to hike along a marked-out track through the surrounding forest and tick off as many things as we could from a list of items we needed to spot. For each item we had to describe it in a few sentences to prove that we'd seen it. Each item was worth a number of points. But the most important rule was that every member of each cabin group had to cross the finish line together. The group with the most points would be named the winner!

'We can win this!' hissed Johnno. 'I know we can!'

Each cabin group took off from the starting line at our campsite in five-minute intervals. We were the third team in line.

'GO!' shouted the teachers.

Johnno and I sprinted as if we were being chased by a **man-eating lion**. Marty and Tubs struggled to keep up. Both had good excuses. Marty was assigned to carry the record sheet and pen — so that made it very hard to run. And Tubs, well, he had a lot of extra weight, namely his belly, to carry.

'Wait up!' yelled Marty. 'We've missed the first item!'

We stopped to ask him what it was.

'An old yellow sign!'

'Here it is!' shouted Tubs, pointing in the grass.

We all ran back to Tubs and Marty ticked off the item on the sheet. He then described the sign: 'It's yellow with a picture of a red bulldozer on it.'

'Right!' announced Johnno. 'First one done. Let's get to the next one!'

We decided to jog and not sprint — so we wouldn't miss any items along the way.

By the fifth item we felt we were unstoppable.

'Hey! Look, a **canoe!**' Johnno said pointing toward the

river, which happened to snake along the hiking track.

The canoe was tied to a log on the bank of the river.

By the time I asked Marty if the canoe was on the list, Johnno and Tubs had gone to take a closer look.

Marty and I reluctantly followed.

'It's not on the list,' Marty said, looking annoyed about leaving the track.

'Where's our next item?' asked Johnno, who was ready to hop into the canoe.

'It's over the bridge,' Marty replied.

We all looked upstream to see the bridge nearby.

'So let's get going,' added Marty. 'Before the other group catches up with us!'

Johnno suggested that since we had to cross the river using the bridge, maybe we could canoe across instead.

No way! protested Marty. 'We'll get in trouble.'

I agreed. But Johnno kept pressuring us.

'Don't be wimps!' he snarled. 'Come on, we're on camp. This is supposed to be fun!'

I don't know how it exactly happened, but somehow

moments later Johnno convinced us to get into the canoe and he pushed us out onto the river. When he jumped in to join us we all suddenly realized we were missing something very important.

'Where are the oars?' croaked Tubs. 'How are we supposed to paddle this thing?!'

We all laughed nervously for a few seconds until we realised we were floating downstream. The river's current was stronger than it looked.

'Start paddling with your hands,' panicked Marty.

We all started to paddle. But it was no use. We weren't getting anywhere. Instead we continued to float downstream — further and further away from the bridge and our hiking track.

'See what **trouble** you've got us in now?' snapped Marty.

'Well, let's swim across!' gulped Johnno, now looking worried.

'I can't swim,' said Tubs.

'And it's almost winter. The water is freezing!' added

Marty. 'We'd all die of hypothermia!'

As Marty and Johnno began to argue with each other about the trouble we were in, I noticed that the current had started flowing much faster — we were now moving at rapid pace.

HEEEEEELLLLLLPPPPP! I shouted.

My friends stopped arguing and realized that my call for help was probably the best idea yet. They joined in with me.

HHEEEEEEEEEEEEELLLLLLLLLPPPP!!

Our voices echoed throughout the national park as we continued to race downstream. But no-one answered. I guessed we had already gone a kilometre or so down the river. We had probably passed the campsite and were heading deep into the wilderness; far away from everyone.

Moments later we were all hanging onto the canoe for our dear lives. The river had turned into wild, choppy killer rapids. We bumped and bounced off rocks as if we were on one of those crazy rides at a water fun park — except

this was **definitely no fun!**

We screamed our heads off.

'AAAAAAAARRRRRRRRRRGGGHHHH!'

I was so scared that I'm sure I broke wind — but I'm also sure the others hadn't heard or smelt it in the **whirlpool of death** we were in.

'We're OK! We're OK!' panted Tubs, his fingers still clenched on either side of the canoe. 'The rough bit is over. It's calm again.'

We were all relieved to see that the mega-terrifying rapids were now behind us. We floated gently for a few moments. It was the slowest the current had been since we hopped in the canoe. Marty suggested we paddle with our hands again. This time we could do it easily and we were finally able to stroke across to the riverbank. We were safe. We couldn't wait to get out of the canoe, happily stumbling onto land.

'Now what?' asked Tubs, looking as if he were about to cry.

It was a good question.

'We walk back along the river's edge, that way we won't get lost,' said Johnno.

'Yeah, good idea,' I added before I caught Marty shaking his head at me.

'Um, didn't you notice that we went through a **massive ravine**?' he said, as if it were the most obvious thing in the world. 'There are huge, steep rocky cliffs along a large part of this river, not to mention the thick bushland. There's no way we can get through all that!'

'So, what ... what are we gonna do?' I stuttered.

'We just have to wait here until they notice that we, and the canoe, are gone,' Marty shrugged calmly. 'In the meantime, we can take cover among the trees over there to get some protection from the cold wind. When the rescue team comes down the river they'll see the canoe tied up here — and they'll find us. So, we'll have to be extremely—'

'Um, Marty,' interrupted Tubs. 'Where's the canoe?'

We whipped our heads around to see the canoe floating downstream.

'**NO!!!**' yelped Marty. 'Why didn't you tie it up?'

'Don't look at me!' snapped Johnno. 'I was the first one to hop out!'

'No you weren't!'

'Yes I was!'

'No, you weren't! It was Tubs. I can't believe you could do this. After getting us into this trouble in the first place...'

'Me! Yeah right, blame it all on me...'

Marty and Johnno broke into a full-on argument and somewhere in the middle of it Tubs and I joined in. Lost in the middle of a national park wilderness we snapped at one another until a **spine-chilling screech** frightened the living poop out of us.

'What was that?' squealed Tubs, practically jumping into my arms.

'It was just some stupid bird,' said Johnno, trying to act brave even though I could tell he was just as frightened as we were.

'Beeeeeep!'

'What's that?' we all asked.

Tubs shoved his hand into his pocket and pulled out a mobile phone.

'YOUR MOBILE PHONE!' we said excitedly.

Tubs smiled.

'Oh, yeah, I forgot I had that,' he said.

'Give that to me,' said Marty, snatching the phone off him. 'I'll call my mum and she'll call the school ... and they'll get help.'

We all smiled again. We knew we were going to be saved now.

'Hello Mum, we're in trouble. You have to call the school because ... Mum? Mum? I don't believe it! The **battery's flat**. It's dead!'

For the next few moments we blamed Tubs for not having a fully-charged phone, and then we moved on to Johnno again for convincing us to get in the canoe. Eventually we all agreed that blaming each other wasn't going to get us anywhere. We knew we had to be patient and hope that someone would come to find us.

We all moved away from the river and made our way into the forest. It was dark and spooky, so we hadn't ventured in very far. We found a little cleared-out area and sat against a fallen tree.

Huddled together like frightened rabbits we waited. Marty tried to make a fire by rubbing two sticks together, but he couldn't. Tubs talked about how hungry he was and that he would pass out any second if he didn't eat soon. Johnno told us about a movie he saw about how these kids were stranded on an island without any food and then they decided to **eat one another**, which made us all very nervous, especially Tubs — he did have the most meat on him.

Hours passed and before we knew it, it was dark — and still no-one had come to rescue us. We were all very scared and cold. Marty said we'd all be warmer if we got in closer to one another — to create some body heat he said. It sort of worked. And then...

'**PHWWWOOHH!**' everyone groaned.

'That was foul!' complained Johnno. 'That's all we need!'

'Sorry,' I said. 'I'd been holding it in for hours!'

'Well, hold the rest of them in,' added Marty.

'Actually, it felt kind of warm,' said Tubs, who was closest to me. 'It was **gross but warm!**'

'Ewww, you're sick Tubs,' scoffed Johnno.

A few moments later I uncontrollably let another silent but deadly one rip.

'PPHHWWWWWWOOOOHHHH!'

'Ben, if you're gonna keep doing that, you have to leave the group!' ordered Marty.

'I can't help it,' I said. 'I need to go to the toilet!'

'Then go!' everyone replied.

My friends told me to go and do it behind a tree. And I was going to, until Johnno started talking about wild animals that would attack me from out of the darkness and **bite me on the butt**.

So I stayed. That's until I passed gas again. And this time even I thought it was pretty rotten. I decided I would go back to the riverbank and try to go to the toilet there.

When I got there I made my way on to some rocks by the river's edge. I squatted and pulled down my pants. I'd been dying to go all day long.

But suddenly out of nowhere I was startled by this bright light. It was a giant spotlight that was aimed right at me. I was stunned and didn't know which way to look. I realized I was **lit up** like a Christmas tree **with my pants down** around my ankles.

'WE FOUND THEM!' I heard a voice say, coming from upstream.

    ❁   ❁   ❁   ❁

When the rescue boat returned us to safety, my friends and I were blinded by bright lights from the TV news cameras — while our parents, teachers, classmates and the ambulance officers rushed to our sides. A search-and-rescue team had been looking for us for hours. We knew we'd face the music in the morning, for getting into that canoe in the first place, but for now everyone was relieved and happy to see that we were all OK.

As the ambulance officers checked us out, I caught Tubs, Marty and Johnno grinning at me.

'What?' I mouthed to them.

'If it wasn't for your rotten stinkers we wouldn't have been found,' said Marty.

'Yeah, well, you're welcome,' I said, **proud** for the first time in my life **to have been gassy**. 'But I'm still busting to go!'

We all laughed. Our ordeal was over.

Once I hung up from speaking to my cousin David, I made my way to bed. Aaaahh, bed ... safe, warm, a-million-miles-away-from-camp, bed. What a day. I will never forget it and ...

PHWWWOOHH!

OK, enough's enough! I really have to go to the toilet.

IV.

PHWWWOOH!

AGAIN!

THE STICK-DUDES COMIC
VERSION

...YEAH...I'M OKAY! I'M GLAD TO BE HOME... SO YOU SAW ME ON TV...

...WELL... IT ALL BEGAN WHEN MY CLASSMATES AND I WERE ON A BUS HEADING TO CAMP...

SO IT WAS YOU! IT WAS YOU THAT GASSED OUT THE BUS!

IT'S TRUE. IT WAS ME ALL ALONG. I'M THE BIG STINKER! I'LL TRY TO KEEP IT A GAS-FREE CABIN — I PROMISE.

GOOD! BECAUSE DUDE, YOUR BUTT-BURPS ARE NASTY!

HEY, GUYS...THE TEACHERS ARE CALLING US FOR OUR FIRST CAMP ACTIVITY... ORIENTATION HIKE RACE!

STUDEN

VI.

Far ~~Cartoons~~

Version 2

a.k.a. famous movies with a stinky twist!

KUNG POO PANDA

SMELL-E

THE CHRONICLES OF NARNIA: PRINCE GASPIAN

GET FART

BRAVEFART

2 FARTS 2 FURIOUS

iNKFART

THE GODFARTER

(THIS ONE IS FOR YOUR FOLKS AND YOUR GRANDPARENTS)

MADAGASCAR

STINKERBELL

VII. FELIX FIBBLY'S FOO-FOO DILEMMA

Felix Fibbly was a worrywart. He worried about everything.

This morning he woke up and got out of bed an hour before his alarm clock was set to go off.

Immediately he began worrying: Had he slept enough? Did he suffer from sleep problems? Would he be able to make up that extra hour tonight? But that would mean he'd have to go to bed early, which would mean he'd miss his favourite show on TV...

And that's not the half of it! Would he have enough energy to get through school today? What if he felt tired during the maths test and fell asleep in the middle of it? Felix hadn't even had breakfast, and already his worrisome mind was working overtime.

When he got to school some of his classmates were wrestling one another, directly in front of where he hung his bag. Oh no, thought Felix. How would he get past them? What if they pulled him into their wrestling game and put him in a headlock? He wouldn't be able to breathe, and if he couldn't breathe, he'd collapse and fall into a coma.

Felix started to pant heavily and nervously chew at his fingernails. He forced himself to shuffle toward his school bag hook without drawing any attention to himself.

'Hey, Fibbly,' called Brandon, one of the boys wrestling who had now caught sight of Felix. **Pull my finger!**

'No thanks,' said Felix, worrying if he should've said yes instead.

'Come on!' pressed Brandon, grinning to his mates. 'Just pull it.'

'But what if I catch germs or something?' croaked Felix. And end up with a killer disease, he thought to himself.

'I'll give you more than germs if you don't hurry up and do it,' growled Brandon, now waving his fist.

Felix reluctantly pulled his finger.

BBBRRRRRRPPPPPPPP!!!!!!

Brandon and his friends burst out laughing as he let rip the massive stinker.

'That's gross,' groaned Felix, who was now worried he was going to pass out. And hit his head on the hard, tiled floor. Another ticket to the hospital!

'It's not gross,' said Brandon, snorting uncontrollably. 'It's human! My dad says it's a sign of **good health**. If you can't get all that gas out of your guts it could cause real problems with your bowels.'

'Bowels?' stuttered Felix.

'Yeah, your intestines in your belly,' added Brandon. 'And if you have bowel problems, then you can really get sick. You can even die from it. So, fart proudly, Fibbly!'

Brandon and his friends slunk off to class, leaving Felix to ponder what had just been said.

Thinking wasn't a good thing for Felix, as it inevitably turned to worrying. Now Felix worried about passing gas. When did he last foo-foo?

Foo-foo was Felix's way of saying fart. He worried if he actually said 'fart' he would upset and offend people — and he certainly didn't want to do that.

For the rest of the day, Felix worried about not being able to foo-foo.

'What if Brandon is right?' he said to himself while strolling home after school. '**I haven't foo-fooed** for hours. Come to think of it, I don't think I foo-fooed yesterday, either. Not even a tiny one.'

Now Felix was really worried. He was so worried he couldn't worry about anything else. As far as he was concerned he had to foo-foo, quick smart.

When he got home he rushed into the kitchen and flung open the pantry. 'Right, where is it? Where, where, where!? Ah, gotcha!' he said, reaching for a can of **baked beans**.

In no time at all Felix had made himself a plate of baked beans on toast. If anything was going to solve his foo-foo dilemma, then this delicious snack definitely would.

Everyone knows that certain foods are better than others when it comes to producing gas. And Felix was sure that beans were at the top of that list.

'Well, someone must be hungry,' said Felix's mother, coming in from the other room. 'I thought I could smell toast. Is everything OK, love?'

'It will be,' mumbled Felix with his mouth full. 'And it won't be toast you'll be smelling soon.'

'Well, take it easy. The way you're scoffing that down, you'll get indigestion,' she added.

Normally Felix would worry about his mum's last comment. But he only had one thing on his mind. He had to foo-foo soon or else **he might die**!

Two hours later, and there was still no movement in Felix's end paddock.

'Oh no,' Felix sighed miserably. 'I can't believe the beans haven't worked. There must be something else that causes people to foo-foo? What am I going to do-do? I mean, do.'

Felix had a thought. He jumped on to the computer and went online to find some help. A few clicks away, he came across a list of things that helped or caused people to pass gas. Felix printed it out.

He read the first item on the list.

Eat beans. Beans contain certain sugars that our intestines do not process well. The bacteria go crazy, causing us to produce **lots of gas**.

'Yeah right,' thought Felix. 'Not for me they don't. I can cross that one off.'

Felix read the next thing on the list.

Go flying. When you're in a low-pressure environment like an aeroplane cabin, the gases in the stomach expand, causing you to pass wind.

Felix instantly thought of his dad. He was a helicopter pilot in the army. He had been away for six months and Felix missed him terribly.

'Well, I wish I were with him,' Felix sighed. 'Then we'd be able to foo-foo together!'

Felix read on.

Drink soft drink. Carbonated drinks are full of air and have been known to cause gas.

Chew gum or suck on a lolly. When you chew you suck in air. The air can bloat your colon. That can result in wind being passed.

Take a warm bath. This will relax you. When your muscles are totally relaxed your body tends to **expel gas**.

Hmm. I can do all these, thought Felix, already rushing to the fridge to grab a can of cola. Felix swigged the fizzy drink in four large gulps.

'BBBBBUUUUUUUURRRRRPPP!'

'Well, at least I know I can burp,' he thought. 'I just wish the air would come out the **other end!**'

Felix stood by the fridge waiting for the drink to have an effect in the downstairs department. But nothing. Just a couple more burps. No foo-foos.

'Hey, Mum! Do you have any chewing gum?' Felix asked.

'Check my purse!' she yelled back.

Felix rummaged through his mother's purse and luckily

there were two sticks of chewing gum. He hurriedly shoved them both in his mouth and began to chew. He chewed and chewed and chewed.

'Come on!' he urged himself. 'Got to get some air down there.'

Felix chewed for half an hour, until he could chew no longer. His jaw felt like wet cement hardening by the second. He spat out the gum and waited. But still no whiff of a foo-foo — not even when he squeezed and pushed his **butt cheeks** together!

There was only one other thing on the list for Felix to attempt: have a warm bath.

'Felix? Are you OK?' said Mrs Fibbly, knocking on the bathroom door. 'Are you having a bath? I can hear splashing. You usually don't like to take baths for fear of hitting your head and drowning.'

'I'm fine, Mum,' said Felix, who was now lying in hot, soapy, bubbly water, trying desperately to relax.

'Why don't you have the light on? Do you have candles in there?' coughed Mrs Fibbly, peeking through the crack in the door.

'Um . . . yes,' stuttered Felix, a little embarrassed.

'Well that's a bit odd isn't it? Are you sure you're OK?'

'Yes, Mum,' said Felix impatiently, 'I'm just trying to have a peaceful bath here, so if you don't mind . . .'

'Well excuse me. It must be hard being a schoolkid these days . . .' Mrs Fibbly said sarcastically. 'Don't be long. Dinner's soon.'

Felix sighed heavily once he heard his mother walk away.

'Right . . . deep breaths, relax, relax,' Felix exhaled, hoping he would **foo-foo soon**.

Time passed. Felix looked for bubbles of the non-soapy kind. But again, nothing. Absolutely nothing.

'Come on!' Felix groaned.

When the water had cooled until it was just too cold to lie in any longer, Felix hopped out, frustrated and bloated. He was so full of beans and soft drink, but still there was **no release**.

Felix knew it would be impossible to stop worrying about being unable to break wind. Later that night, trying desperately to get it out of his mind, he sat down to watch TV on the couch with his mum. He thought his worries were over when he heard a loud **pop-poppety-pop-pop!**

'Did I just let one rip?' he smiled. 'It didn't really feel as if I did.'

'I'm sorry, love,' said Felix's mother, blushing. 'I thought I could sneak out a quiet one.'

'Oh, thanks Mum, that's just great!' huffed Felix, quickly jumping to his feet.

'Well, I'm sorry, and surprised that you're so offended. You know it's natural for. . .'

'Yeah, I know,' snapped Felix. 'Why couldn't it have been me?!'

Felix stormed out of the room.

A few minutes later, Mrs Fibbly tapped at Felix's bedroom door.

'What was all that about?' she said softly, entering the room.

Felix was lying on his bed with his arms behind his head.

'Are you all right? Felix? What's wrong?'

'Sorry Mum, it's nothing,' Felix mumbled.

'Well, that little outburst you just had, and all that extra worrying you've been doing lately isn't really nothing.'

Felix knew his mother was right. He knew he worried too much ... generally. But this was different! He didn't want **his intestines to explode!** He was too young to die!

'Look,' she added. 'I've booked you in to see someone tomorrow after school. He's a type of doctor, and he'll be able to talk to you about things in a way I can't.'

Felix was going to say no way was he going to see some stranger, but because of the squished and worried look on his mother's face, he decided to just say yes.

The next morning arrived and Felix, as far as he knew, still hadn't broken wind. This made him more anxious than he had ever been in his entire life. When the time came for him to see the doctor, he was beside himself. So much so, that all the things he worried about came flooding out of him. He talked to the doctor non-stop for an entire hour.

Later that evening, Felix overheard his mother talking to his grandmother.

'Yes, the doctor said his worries basically stem from the absence of John ... yeah ... that's what he said, not having his father around plays a big part ... and the therapist also mentioned that at the moment he's worrying about not being able to pass wind. Says he thinks he's going to die from it! Can you believe it? I know ... I know ... poor kid.'

Felix closed his bedroom door. He didn't think of himself as a poor kid. He couldn't see what the problem was. As far as he was concerned, there was nothing wrong with him ... **except for his foo-foo dilemma**.

The following morning, Felix received some wonderful news. His dad was coming home! It was supposed to be a surprise, but his mum couldn't keep it in any longer. She had known for days that he was coming home and finally told Felix over breakfast.

'This is unreal! Great news!' whooped Felix. 'When does he get here?'

'Tonight,' smiled Felix's mother. 'We'll meet him at the airport.'

For the rest of the day Felix thought about his dad so

much that he almost forgot about foo-fooing. But he still kept very detailed notes about his visits to the bathroom, just in case he needed to show a doctor. His stomach felt like a **blown-up balloon**, fit to burst.

Finally the time had come. Felix and his mother waited excitedly at the airport. 'There he is!' shouted Felix, pointing at his father as he came through the sliding doors in the arrivals hall.

Felix and his mother rushed to Mr Fibbly and hugged him tightly.

'Let me push your luggage, Dad,' Felix insisted, as they started to make their way to the car.

As Felix and his parents stepped into the lift that would take them to the floor where their car was parked, an alarm bell suddenly rang, followed by a thump. The lift had stopped.

'What's going on? I think we're stuck!?' said a boy whose family was sharing the lift with the Fibblies.

'Give it a few seconds,' said Mr Fibbly, as if he knew all about lifts. 'Should start up again soon.'

But a few seconds turned into a few minutes and everyone began to **panic** slightly — everyone except Felix. Yes, Felix, worrywart of the century, was cool as a cucumber. He even surprised himself with how laid-back he was.

'Um, hello,' he said calmly into the emergency phone in the lift. 'Yes ... we're stuck in a lift ... yeah, between the third and fourth floors ... yeah, that's right ... the B wing parking lot ... Thanks.'

Felix hung up the phone. 'It won't be much longer now,' he said, looking up at his dad and smiling.

Just then, Felix felt something strange. His stomach began to **rumble** and **gurgle** the same way it did when he needed to make an emergency visit to the toilet. Suddenly, without any warning at all ...

BBBBBRRRRRRRPPPPPPPPPP!!!!!!

Felix had done a massive, ear-shattering foo-foo!

The other family groaned while Mr and Mrs Fibbly chuckled nervously. 'Oh, son, you could've waited!' grinned Mr Fibbly, ruffling Felix's hair.

'No, Dad, there was no way I was going to wait any longer.'

Not only had Felix's foo-foo been a loud one, it was also **very potent**. He didn't notice the other family in the lift holding their hands to their noses, coughing and spluttering loudly. He was just so happy to have one less thing to worry about!

When the lifts were eventually opened, everyone stepped out in a hurry. The lift technicians copped some of the **residual stink** and quickly tried to shut the doors again!

Later that evening in bed, Felix smiled, knowing his father was back safe, and that his bowels weren't going to blow up.

Throughout the night Felix foo-fooed at least **twenty times** under the covers. The next morning he woke up without a worry in the world... Although he did notice a strange itch on his arm that he thought might be chickenpox, or perhaps even a flesh-eating organism that might be burrowing its way to his brain, or...

VII.
FARTICUS MAXIMUS:
SILENTUS BUT DEADLIUS

PARTUS ONE

MEGA-TRIPLE-WHAMMY-STINK BOMB!

'What do we do now?' worried Farticus.

'We have to join together!' exclaimed Gassius.

'Otherwise these blood-sucking beasts are going to **eat us alive**.'

Gassius sidled up next to Farticus.

'For now we are not enemies, my fellow stinker,' he

whispered. 'For now we are brothers and we will have
to let 'em rip like we've never let 'em rip before. Are you
ready to unleash the
windus within us?'

'Yep, I'm ready,'
nodded Farticus.
'Let the games
begin!'

It was the lions
and tigers that
charged first.

'NOW!' shouted Gassius.

BBBRRRRRRPPPPPPPP!!!!!!

Farticus and Gassius popped off in unison. It was a thunderous cracker. Combined, their deadly rotten windus was a powerful **super-explosive weapon**. It hurled the big cats five metres off the ground. They were out cold by the time they landed.

Next came the wolves. Followed by the rhinos and the bulls.

Farticus and Gassius released a **mega-triple-whammy-stink-bomb** of a ripper. The wolves were knocked out unconscious within seconds, the bulls crashed head first into the ground and the horns of the rhinos crumbled into pieces like crushed almond cookies.

The crowd had not seen anything like it before. The gas in the stadium was so thick and so rotten that many of the spectators had broken out in **coughing fits**. Even with their orange-scented snotus-rags they could still smell the deadly gut-busting stench.

'Farticus, we've gotta get out of here!' said Gassius, as he watched the grizzly bears making their move. 'That **two-faced evilus emperor** is probably going to hit us with something else!'

Farticus looked up into the crowd. He could see that Emperor Bullius was not happy. In fact, he looked utterly furious. Gassius was right. They had to get out of there.

'You try to hold the bears off!' yelled Farticus as he ran back to the gate that led to his changing cell. 'I'll work out an escape plan for us!'

'No problemus!' nodded Gassius. 'I feel a real gem is about to pop any second now!'

'Sinus!' Farticus called out.

'That was absolutely marvellous!' exclaimed Sinus as he emerged from out of the shadows at the gate. 'The way you two dealt with those rhinos ... woah, **that was special!**'

'We have no time for that!' puffed Farticus. 'It's obvious that Emperor Bullius wants to butterfly-kiss both Gassius and me. We have to get out of here. Go get Rhina, my mother, and the boys. Now! We have no time to waste, we have …'

Sinus, we have to get out of here! Go get Rhina, my mother and the boys! Now!

'ARRRGGGGGHHHH!!!'

The crowd screamed and gasped.

Farticus turned to see that Gassius had been pinned down by one of the grizzly bears.

'Let's go now, Farticus!' cried Sinus, tugging at his arm. 'Don't worry about Gassius, it's **too late for him!**

'I can't leave him here!' croaked Farticus, shrugging away from Sinus. 'He needs my help. Just go and get the others!'

Farticus sprinted back toward Gassius and the grizzly bears.

PARTUS TWO

THUMP, THUMP, THUMPITY, THUMP!

When Farticus reached Gassius, the biggest of the bears was sprawled directly on top of him. The bear was smothering him to death. Farticus could see that Gassius was **struggling to break windus**. The weight of the giantus grizzly against his stomach prevented him from being able to squeeze out even a little fluffy, much less a powerful ripper.

139

The other nine bears encircled Gassius. They then turned to face Farticus as if daring him to try and break through. Farticus slowly took a few steps back and then **sprinted toward the bears**.

The crowd were now in hysterics. They screamed, cheered and stomped their feet. Farticus took a giantus leap, flew through the air, and

BBBRRRRRRPPPPPPPP!!!!!!

His wind blew the three closest bears clean away, causing them to butt heads as they came crashing down to the ground. The other six bears roared angrily and charged at Farticus all at once. Farticus whipped around and again,

BBBRRRRRRRPPPPPPPP!!!!!!

The rest of the bears all hit the arena with a thump, thump, thumpity, thump! Farticus hugged them one by one with his sword.

Now for the gruesome grizzly on top of Gassius.

Farticus jumped on top of the bear and grabbed him in a headlock. The bear bolted upright, growling and groaning angrily. Gassius was finally free. He was badly injured, having been bitten several times on the arms and legs. Blood was everywhere. Farticus released his grip on the bear and dashed back to the wounded Gassius.

'Are you OK?' asked Farticus. The gladiators now faced the last **furious furry opponent** together.

'Yeah, just. I thought I was a goner. You saved my life. I will never forget this,' croaked Gassius. 'So, you ready to double up and blow this giantus furball away?'

'Ready when you are!'

As the bear charged, Farticus and Gassius together released two of the most potent farts of the afternoon — **double SBDs** — Silentus but Deadliusses.

The bear ran right into the cloud of stink and froze for several seconds. Its eyes rolled back and then . . .

SLAPPED BY A SILENTUS BUT DEADLIUS

PHWOOMP!! It collapsed to the ground with an almighty whack. And again the stadium erupted with wild cheers.

'Let's get out of here!' shouted Farticus, noticing that Emperor Bullius had just ordered a squadron of armed soldiers into the arena.

The chase was on.

Farticus took Gassius by the arm and sprinted for the gate where he had left Sinus.

'Let me go!' groaned Gassius. 'I'm slowing you down. Bullius's men are going to catch us any second now!'

'Come on! **We're almost there!**' panted Farticus as he and Gassius disappeared into the tunnel underneath the Colosseum.

They bolted along the dark stone corridors. The clanging armour of the soldiers echoed behind them.

By order of the emperor, stop those two stinkeruses!

'Where are they? I told Sinus to meet us here!' gasped Farticus as he and Gassius burst onto a piazza outside the Colosseum.

'Farticus! Gassius!'

Farticus turned to see Rhina, Sinus, his mother, and the boys dashing toward them.

'Are you OK?!' cried Rhina, throwing her arms around Farticus. 'What's going on? I can't believe the emperor set you up! Is he really out to butterfly-kiss you both?'

'Yes, it's all true, but we don't have time to explain, my dearus. Any second now the soldiers will be here! Which

way do we go, Gassius? How do we get out of this city?'

'I don't know, I'm from Britannia, remember?' gulped Gassius. 'Emperor Bullius will no doubt block off every street with his troops. We need to find a secret way out. Sinus, do you know one?'

Sinus shrugged. As did Rhina and Farticus's mother.

'What are we going to do?' said Odorus and Stinkius in unison.

'Let's take them on!' shouted Rotteneggus, punching his fist into his palm.

'Look!' said Farticus's mother, pointing toward two teenage boys running toward them.

We can help you get out of here! My name is Cornelius and this is my cousin, Rufus. I know this city like the back of my handus!

'**We can help you!**' cried the older of the two. 'My name is Cornelius and this is my cousin, Rufus. I know this city like the back of my handus. I can get you out of here.'

Lead the way kind boys!

'Then lead the way, kind boys!' said Farticus. 'We have no timus to waste! Get us outta here, now!'

Cornelius and Rufus led them down a side alley only moments before Emperor Bullius's soldiers charged out onto the piazza.

The smelly gladiators had **got away!**

WILL FARTICUS AND HIS FAMILY GET OUT OF ROME
SAFELY, ESCAPING THE EVIL CLUTCHES OF EMPEROR
BULLIUS AND HIS ARMY?

WILL GASSIUS KEEP HIS EYES OFF RHINA?

FIND OUT IN THE NEXT RIP-ROARING,
FARTASTIC EPIC. . .

FARTICUS MAXIMUS:
BOTTOMUS BURPS OF BRITANNIA

(AND OTHER FOUL-SMELLING STORIES!)

MORE HILARIOUS ADVENTURES FROM BEST-SMELLING AUTHOR FELICE ARENA!

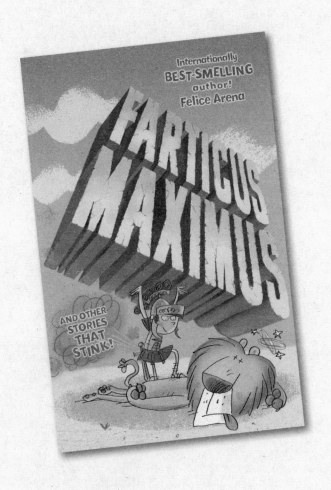

Visit www.farticusmaximus.com.au

MORE HILARIOUS ADVENTURES
FROM BEST-SELLING
AUTHOR FELICE ARENA